THE GREAT NEW ZEALAND MOA HUNT

Written and illustrated by

Michael Salmon

Puffin Books

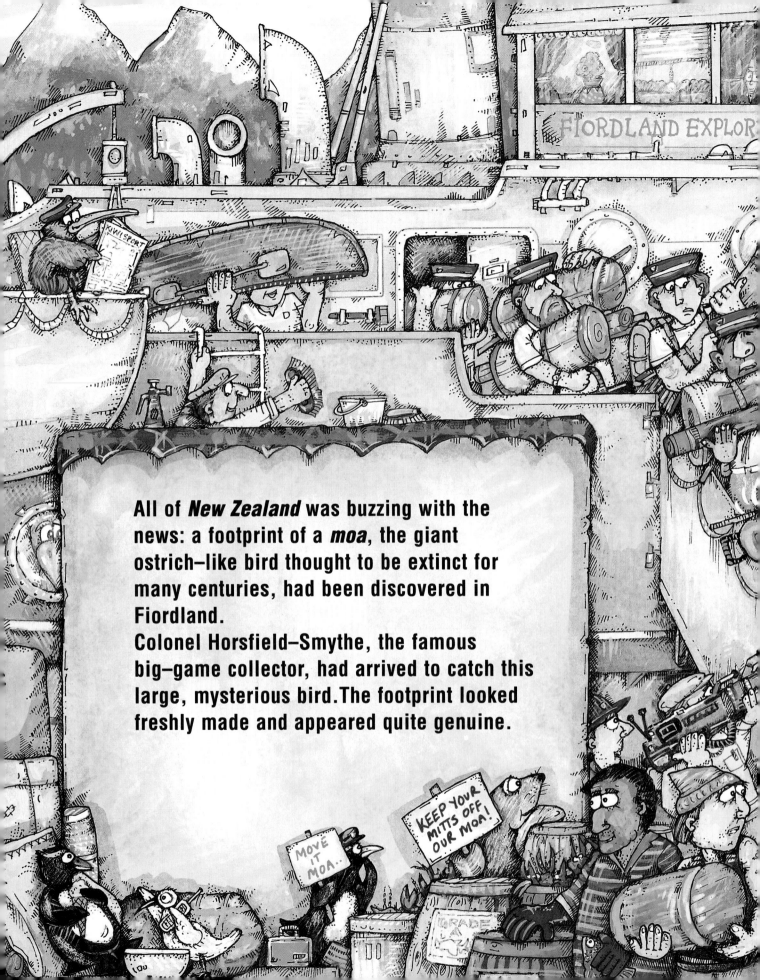

All of *New Zealand* was buzzing with the news: a footprint of a *moa*, the giant ostrich–like bird thought to be extinct for many centuries, had been discovered in Fiordland.

Colonel Horsfield–Smythe, the famous big–game collector, had arrived to catch this large, mysterious bird. The footprint looked freshly made and appeared quite genuine.

That night a gala dinner was held in honour of the Colonel. There hadn't been such excitement in the South Island since the Gold Rush.

After some very long speeches a special dessert was carried in. It was a magnificent moa, sculpted in cheesecake, sitting in chocolate custard and decorated with slices of kiwifruit.

TRAMPING TRACK

Early the next morning the Colonel loaded up his three helpers with heavy packs. They left at dawn and headed off into the mountains. The Colonel carried a map showing where the moa print had been found. He had his butterfly net ready — just in case.

It started to rain and by the time they reached the spot
where the moa print had been sighted there was
nothing but *MUD, MUD, MUD*.
The Colonel was very grumpy and retreated to his
warm tent. He was even more determined now to find
that pesky bird.

SQUAWK, SQUAWK

A shrill, screeching noise woke the camp.
The Colonel grabbed his net and flung the tent flap
back. 'It's the *moa*,' he shouted as he dashed off into
the darkness. The Colonel lunged towards some
bushes. '*Got you, moa!*' he yelled, excitedly.

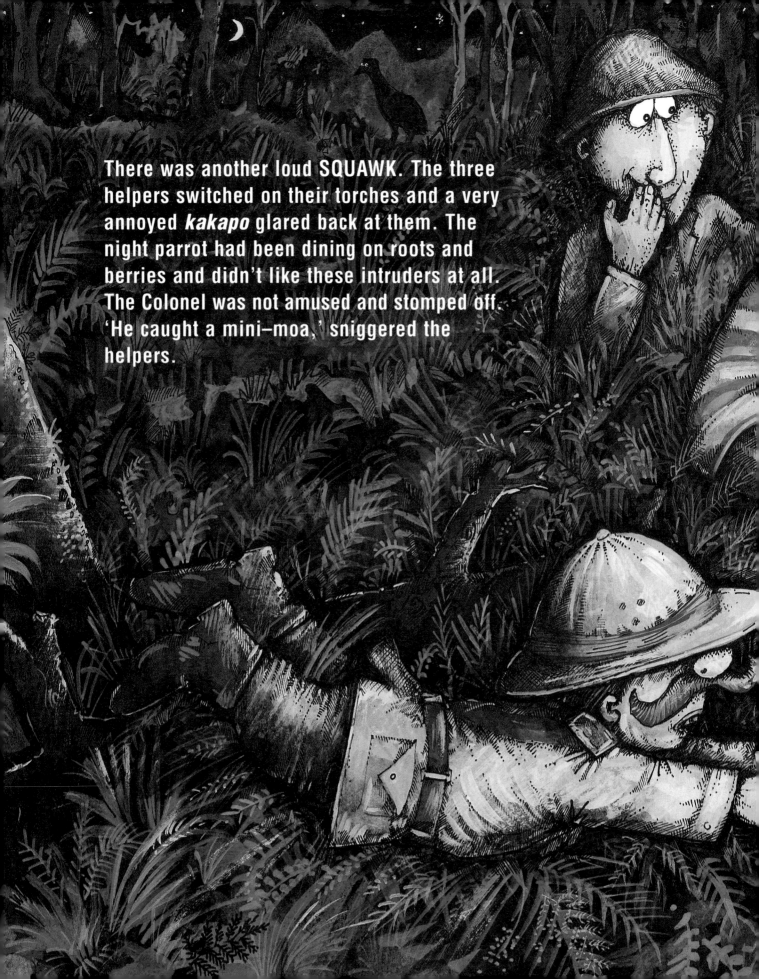

There was another loud SQUAWK. The three helpers switched on their torches and a very annoyed *kakapo* glared back at them. The night parrot had been dining on roots and berries and didn't like these intruders at all. The Colonel was not amused and stomped off. 'He caught a mini–moa,' sniggered the helpers.

By the next morning, the rain had stopped.
The Colonel emerged from his tent holding
a large sheet of paper. 'Men! I have a plan.
You'll build a cage and bait the trap with
sweet–corn fritters.'

The cage was pulled up into a tree and they hid well back in the bush. They waited for hours, as the fritter smell wafted up over the mountain ridges.

Just as he was about to give up, the Colonel saw some movement. He whispered excitedly, 'I can see *one, two, three, four* moa, and YES, they're eating the bait!'

The rope was pulled and the cage came crashing down over four very surprised *chamois goats*, out on their morning stroll. 'Hummph!' the Colonel snorted and once again stalked off angrily.
The helpers released the goats quickly and munched what was left of the tasty fritters.
'Woolly moa, with horns! What next?'
The Colonel returned with his radar tracker; this hunt was getting very serious.

The radar tracker beeped as the antenna spun
and pointed towards a thick clump of ferns.
'Quick! Hand me my net,' demanded the Colonel
rudely. He brushed the ferns aside and there,
sleeping amongst the fronds, was an extremely
large *wild boar*. Its razor–sharp tusks gleamed
in the sun. The boar woke with a start and the
helpers fled for their lives down the ridge,
splashing into a mountain stream on the way.
It was *F-R-E-E-Z-I-N-G.*

'Atishhoo!' sneezed the Colonel as he unrolled another plan. He was getting desperate. He knew that everyone in New Zealand was expecting him to find a moa.

The helpers dug a deep pit and covered it with ferns, twigs and leaves. Carefully, the Colonel pushed a plate of smelly onion and whitebait sandwiches into the centre of the pit.

The Colonel and his helpers climbed up into a tree and rested on its branches, high above the pit. It was getting dark.

The helpers started to feel sleepy but the Colonel remained very alert. Unfortunately, he was looking the other way when a *kiore* bit him on the finger — he had disturbed a family of native rats.

'*Yee-ouch!*' yelled the Colonel but the kiore wouldn't let go of his finger. He grabbed at the nearest helper and overbalanced.

CRACK The branch broke and a tangled mess of branches, leaves, twigs, rats, helpers — and the Colonel — crashed down into the trap. Luckily the ferns over the pit broke their fall.

Colonel Horsfield–Smythe and his helpers limped back in silence,
nursing twisted ankles, cuts, bruises, sore heads and aching backs.
They were disappointed and exhausted.
The Colonel had had enough of Fiordland and its wildlife.
'Be assured New Zealand, the *MOA* is definitely an extinct species —
if one had been around, *I WOULD CERTAINLY HAVE CAUGHT IT,*' he
told the waiting reporters and television cameras.

As the boat steamed back along the Sound, the Colonel stood on the stern deck, gazing up at the towering cliffs with their cascading waterfalls and dense forests.

'Fiordland certainly would be the kind of place a moa could live in and remain hidden from the outside world — if such creatures really did still exist,' he mumbled to himself.

MOA species order *Dinornithiformes*

An extinct giant bird that lived only in New Zealand. The moa ranged in size from those as big as a large turkey, to some that stood more than two and a half metres high and weighed up to 230 kilograms.

The moa was the tallest bird that ever lived. It could not fly and ate green plants and trees. The moa lived undisturbed for over two million years without fear of predators.

The arrival of humans in New Zealand about 1,000 years ago was catastrophic for these huge birds. They were hunted for food, and by the nineteenth century, the largest kinds of moa had disappeared.

The last sighting of a live moa was in about 1850.